For Don and Mary, who make
every moment count
—KD

For Anna Catherine Keane
—JM

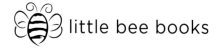 little bee books

A division of Bonnier Publishing
853 Broadway, New York, New York 10003
Text copyright ©2016 by Kristy Dempsey
Illustrations copyright © 2016 by Jane Massey
All rights reserved, including the right of reproduction
in whole or in part in any form. LITTLE BEE BOOKS is a
trademark of Bonnier Publishing Group, and associated colophon is
a trademark of Bonnier Publishing Group.
Manufactured in China   LEO 0416
First Edition
2 4 6 8 10 9 7 5 3 1
Library of Congress Cataloging-in-Publication Data
is available upon request.
ISBN 978-1-4998-0229-0

littlebeebooks.com
bonnierpublishing.com

Ten Little Fingers, Two Small Hands

by Kristy Dempsey   illustrated by Jane Massey

little bee books

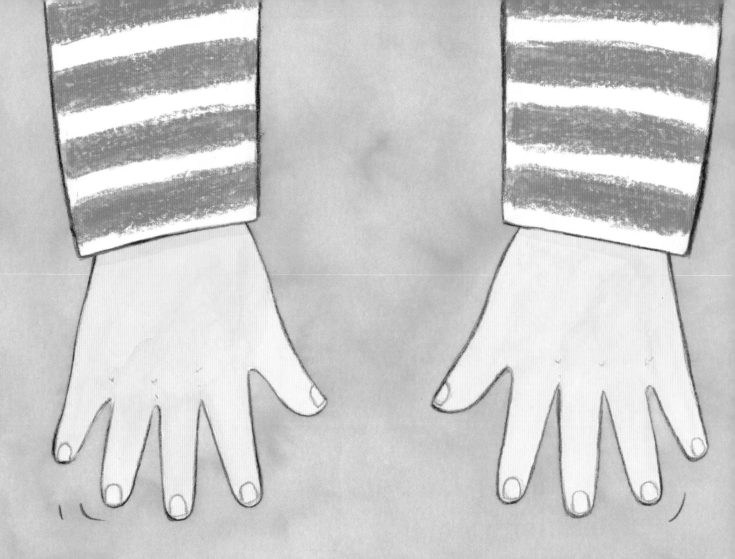

Ten little fingers, one hand...two.

Two small hands belong to you!

Two small hands
have so much fun!

Count each finger one by one.

One little finger points to cake.

Two little fingers tap a plate.

Three little fingers pinch a bite.

Four little fingers squish it tight.

Five little fingers,
quickly done.

Six little fingers, one by one.

Seven little fingers
pour a puddle.

Eight little fingers make a muddle.

Nine little fingers,
clean and dry.

Ten little fingers clap up high!

Two small hands just like before. Then...

one little finger asks for more!

Two hands held together: "Please!"

Two hands stretch and two hands squeeze.

One last bite, then arms up high!

Wash two hands and pat them dry.

Kiss ten fingers,
one hand...two.

Two small hands on
one small you!